GOT JOKED!

by
Ian MacDonald
&
Marc Ellerby

Titles in Once Upon *Another* Time...

PRINCESS FROG-SNOGGER
BY TOMMY DONBAVAND & MARK PENMAN

LITTLE RED
BY BARRY HUTCHISON & MARK PEARCE

THE LEAGUE OF ENCHANTED HEROES
BY TIM COLLINS & JAMES LAWRENCE

THE BOY WHO CRIED ALIENS!
BY DANNY PEARSON & ABBY RYDER

GOLDIE LOCKED!
BY IAN MACDONALD & MARC ELLERBY

ED AND THE SHIRTMAKERS
BY ANDY SEED & RACHAEL SMITH

Badger Publishing Limited
Oldmedow Road,
Hardwick Industrial Estate,
King's Lynn PE30 4JJ

Telephone: **01438 791037**
www.badgerlearning.co.uk

2 4 6 8 10 9 7 5 3 1

Goldie Locked!
ISBN 978-1-78464-526-7

Text © Ian MacDonald 2016
Complete work © Badger Publishing Limited 2016

Publisher: Susan Ross
Senior Editor: Danny Pearson
Editorial Coordinator: Claire Morgan
Illustration: Marc Ellerby
Designer: Fiona Grant

Contents

Characters

Detective Inspector Badger

Detective Sophie Squirrel

The Three Bears

Goldie

Vocabulary

cottage	porridge
detective	sprayed
favourite	splattered
glancing	staggered
muttering	unusual

Once Upon Another Time...

Chapter One
Crime Scene

Detective Inspector Badger here.

Twenty years in the Woodland Police. I thought I'd seen everything.

Until today!

"I'm Detective Inspector Badger," I began, "and this is Detective Sophie Squirrel."

I glanced around at the simple wooden furniture, the blue-striped china bowls, the 56-inch flat-screen TV on the wall.

Nothing unusual... apart from the break in.

"So, what can you tell us about the break in?" asked the squirrel.

"Each morning we go out to collect berries... then it happens," said Mr Bear.

"And just look at the mess!" said Mrs Bear, wiping her hands on her son's head.

I looked.

A gloopy, grey puddle oozed across the tablecloth.

I dipped my finger in and licked.

Porridge! Porridge was something I'd never understood.

"But you say nothing is missing?" asked Sophie.

"It's always the same," Mrs Bear went on, "porridge on the table, a broken chair..."

I looked. There was a pile of broken chairs in the corner, all held together by nails, bits of string... and bubble gum. Pink. My favourite!

I made a note to take some back... for clues.

"And that's not all!" squeaked the smallest bear, holding a broken porridge bowl in his tiny paw. "Come and see!"

We followed the little bear into the next room.

There were three beds. The sheets were lying, crumpled, on the floor.

Someone had sprayed letters on the wall:

BEARS ARE STUPID
GOLDIE

Just a hunch but maybe this person didn't like bears.

"It's not much to go on," I said, glancing at Sophie, who was chewing a pencil.

"But she's got be stopped!" cried Mrs Bear.

"Mmmffwargh!" said the squirrel. She had just swallowed the pencil whole. "Did you say 'she'? You mean you saw her?"

"Let's sit down and you can tell us what your burglar looked like," I said.

There were no chairs left, so we couldn't sit down.

Sophie found another pencil, and began to draw.

Chapter Two
The Meeting

The next day...

It happened again.

The splattered porridge, another broken chair, the sheets tossed on the floor.

The next day it was the same.

AND THE NEXT.

AND THE NEXT.

Back at the cottage, the bears held a meeting.

"I hate having no breakfast!" cried Baby Bear.

"I hate making the beds every day!" added Mama Bear.

"And I hate mending broken chairs!" said Papa Bear.

"ENOUGH IS ENOUGH!"

They decided to set a trap.

Chapter Three
Goldie?

Later that evening…

A figure crept through the open window.

Three steaming bowls of porridge lay on the table.

She tried the first. Too hot! She tried the second.
Too lumpy! She tried the third.

YAAAAAAARGH!!!

Someone had put extra hot curry powder in it.

The little girl staggered to the sink and plunged her red mouth under the cold water.

She stepped back, knocking over one chair and stubbing her toe on the second. Then, muttering rude words, she sat down on the smallest chair.

"I'll teach those bears to mess with me," she hissed. Goldie stood, ready to slam her body hard into the tiny chair.

But, when she looked, the chair was gone!

It was stuck to her bottom!

With a cry of rage she spun round like a dog chasing its tail. But it was no use.

Instead, she lost her balance and staggered, headfirst, into the bedroom.

She landed on the first bed, bounced off the second and collapsed on the last.

BOING!

The bed snapped shut like the jaws of a crocodile.

"Let me out!"

Later that night...

"We've been looking through our files," began
Sophie.

"That's right," I continued, "And we think Goldie,
here, is not what she seems."

Sophie stepped forward. She tore off the blonde wig...

And peeled back the rubber mask...

"*THE BIG BAD WOLF!*"

The Bear Facts

The story of The Three Bears has been told for more than two hundred years.

The story was first printed in a collection of stories in 1837. Back then, the unwelcome visitor to the bear's house was an old woman!

Bears are not the cuddly animals you see in fairy tales. An adult grizzly can stand up to two and half metres tall. That's scary!

Teddy bears are said to be named after an American President, Theodore 'Teddy' Roosevelt, after he refused to shoot a bear cub on a hunting trip.

In the year 2000, a Stieff teddy bear became the most expensive bear ever – sold at auction for over £125,000!

Many other stories and films have featured famous bears, such as Winnie the Pooh, Paddington and Baloo. Can you think of any others?

Questions

What was the name of the detective squirrel? *(page 4)*

What colour was the bubble gum? *(page 12)*

What was sprayed on the bear's wall? *(page 14)*

How was Goldie trapped? *(page 26)*

Who did Goldie turn out to be? *(page 28)*

Meet the Author

Ian MacDonald began writing while working as a teacher in Kent. His stories are full of weird and wonderful characters... strange aliens, marauding mummies and ghastly gangsters. He shares his writing desk with a cat called Stanley.

Meet the Illustrator

Marc Ellerby lives in Essex where he draws many comics. He has worked on comics for *The Beano*, the BBC and Cartoon Network. He's really into burritos, dog videos and very shouty music.